Dogs Are From Jupiter,
(Cats Are From The Moon)

by SCHULZ

CollinsPublishersSanFrancisco
A Division of HarperCollins*Publishers*

Snoopy
Skins
A Cat

Dogs Are From Jupiter..Cats Are From the Moon

Snoopy Skins A Cat

Snoopy Skins A Cat

Snoopy Skins A Cat

Snoopy Skins A Cat

That Most
Magnificent Of
All Creatures

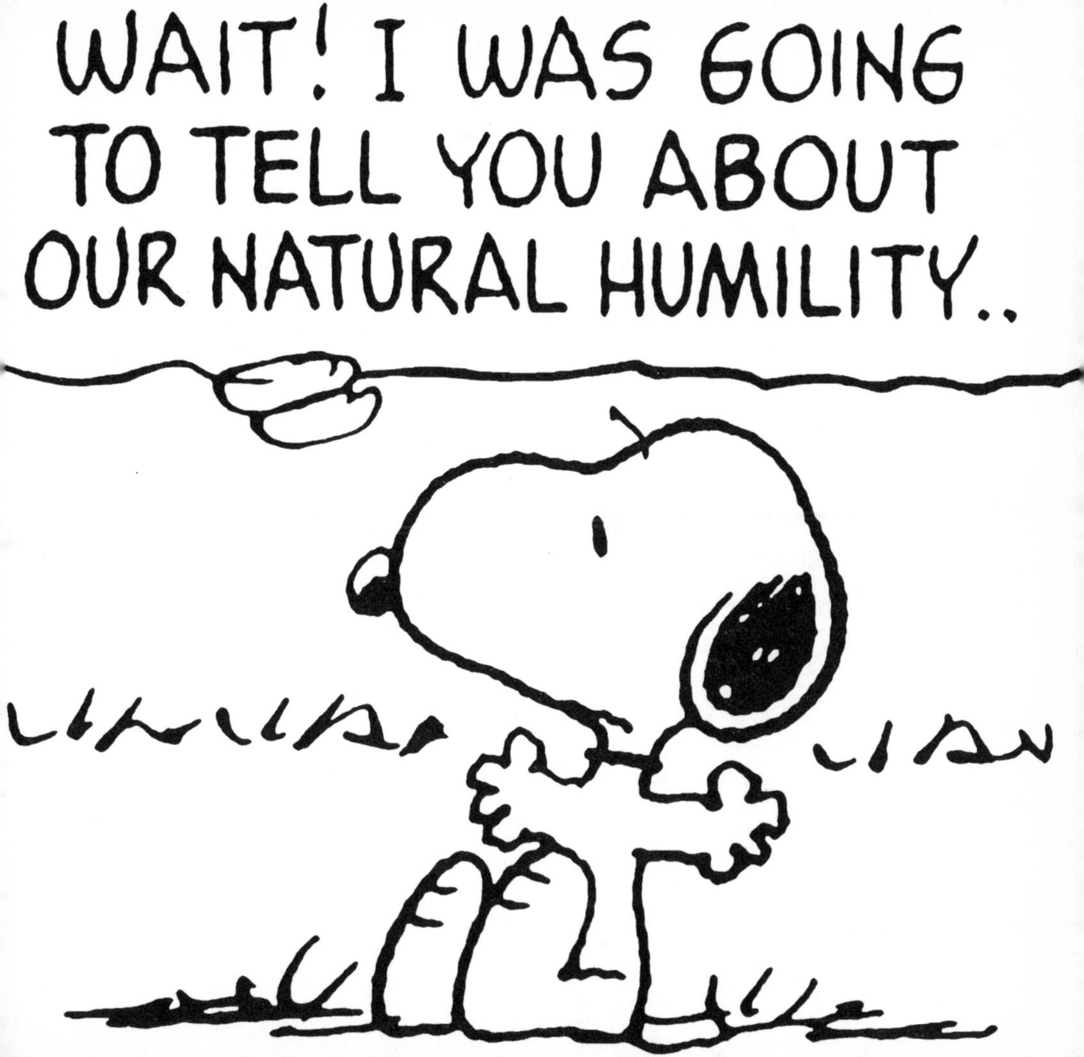
WAIT! I WAS GOING TO TELL YOU ABOUT OUR NATURAL HUMILITY..

Man's Best
Friend?

Man's Best Friend?

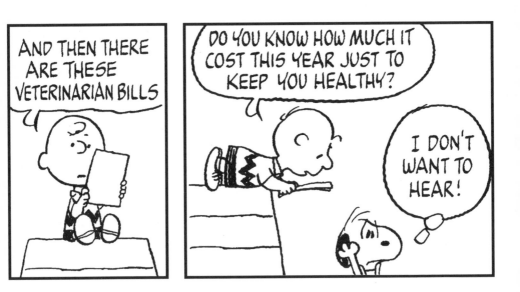

Man's Best Friend?

THIS CAN OF DOG FOOD COST EIGHTY-NINE CENTS..

THIS FROZEN DINNER YOU'RE HAVING TONIGHT COST THREE DOLLARS AND FIFTY CENTS..

MOM AND DAD SHOULD TRADE YOU IN FOR ANOTHER DOG..

 **Man's Best Friend?**

If Dogs Could Talk

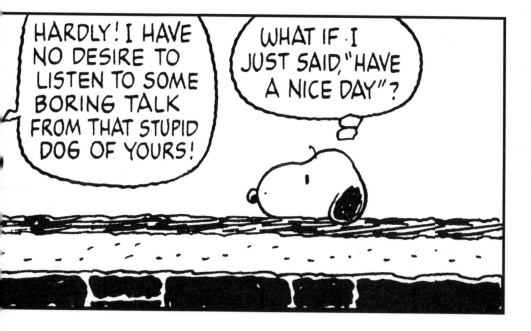

What
Dogs Do
All Day

Z What Dogs Do All Day

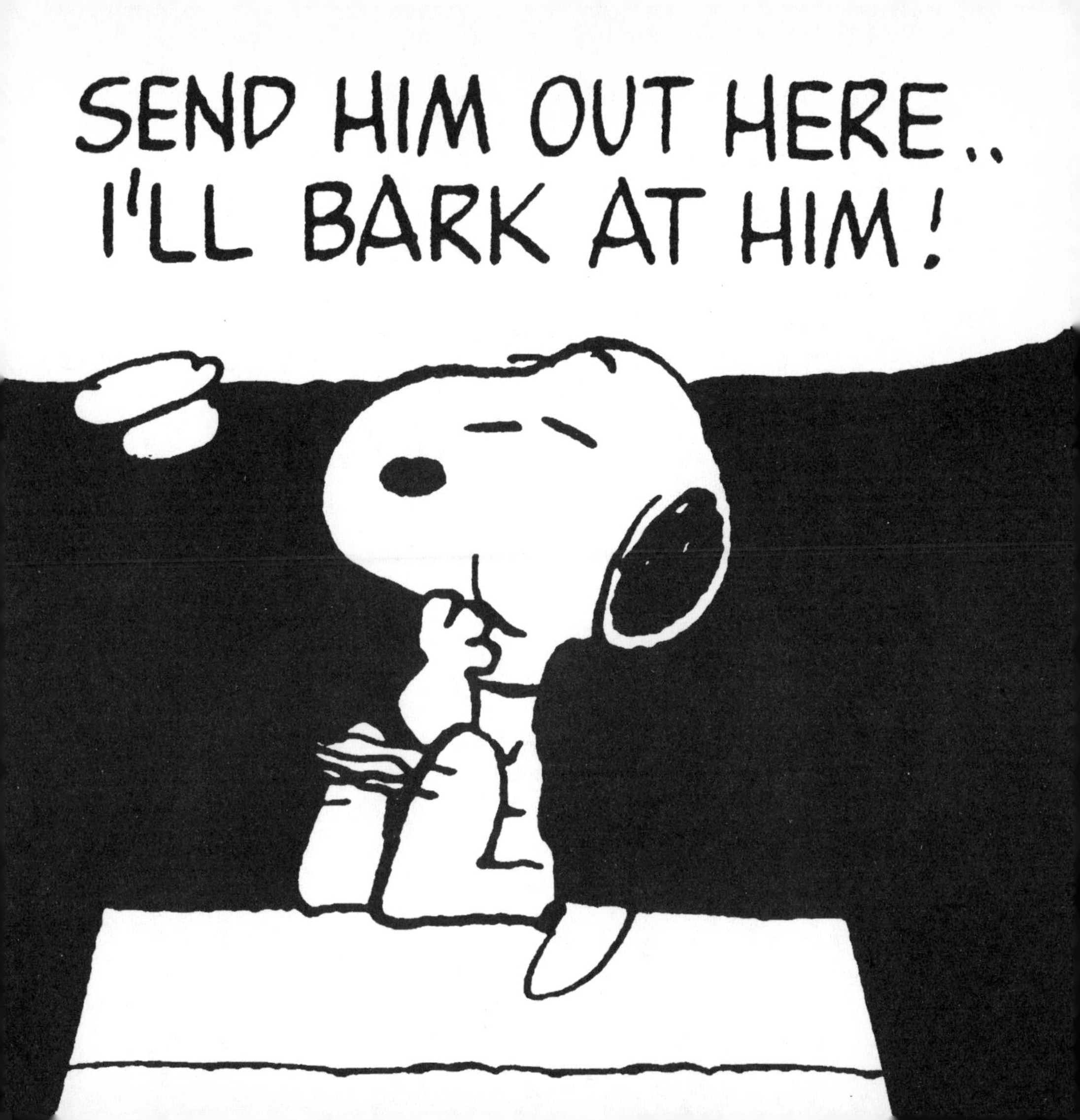
SEND HIM OUT HERE..
I'LL BARK AT HIM!

What Dogs Do All Day

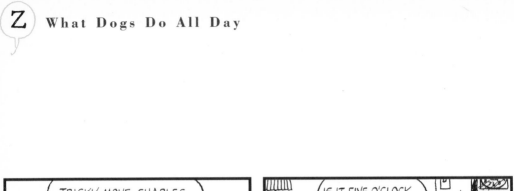

It's
A Dog's
Life

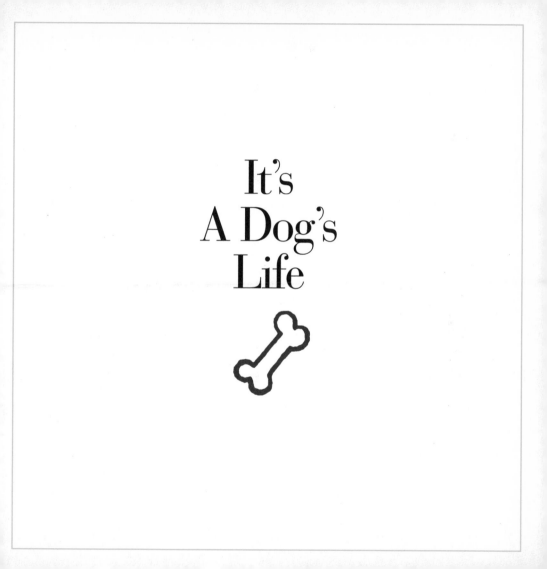

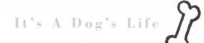

All his life he tried to be a good person.

Many times, however, he failed, for after all, he was only human.

All his life he tried to be a good person.

Many times, however, he failed, for after all, he was only human.

A Packaged Goods Incorporated Book
First published 1996 by Collins Publishers San Francisco
1160 Battery Street, San Francisco, CA 94111-1213
http://www.harpercollins.com
Conceived and produced by Packaged Goods Incorporated
276 Fifth Avenue, New York, NY 10001
A Quarto Company

Library of Congress Cataloging-in-Publication Data
Schulz, Charles M.
[Peanuts. Selections]
Dogs are from Jupiter, cats are from the moon / by Schulz.
p.   cm.
"A Packaged Goods Incorporated Book"—T.p. verso
ISBN 0-00-225208-2
I. Title
PN6728.P4S246   1996
741.5'973—dc20   96-15194
CIP

Printed in Hong Kong

1 3 5 7 9 10 8 6 4 2

ARF!
ARF!

ARF!
ARF!